Four F

A short fiction anthology

Elizabeth Kemball
Sally Filer
Bethany Lewis
Lucy Aur

Four Forked Tongues
Elizabeth Kemball
Sally Filer
Bethany Lewis
Lucy Aur

Brought to you by The Broken Spine

Art and Literature

ISBN: 9798390825020

© Alan Parry, 2023. All rights reserved.

Book design: Alan Parry and Andrew James Lloyd
Cover Art: Elizabeth Kemball
Edited by Alan Parry
All rights to individual texts are held and reserved
by their individual authors.

The Broken Spine Ltd.
Southport / England / United Kingdom
www.thebrokenspine.co.uk

For the truths and lies we each tell to survive.

> "Some are Born to sweet delight
> Some are Born to sweet delight
> Some are Born to Endless Night
> We are led to Believe a Lie…"

William Blake, *Auguries of Innocence*

Contents

1	Poet Cursed - Elizabeth Kemball
11	The Queue and I - Sally Filer
21	Unwoven - Bethany Lewis
31	Heaven is a Coffee Shop - Lucy Aur
38	The Authors
40	Advanced Praise
41	Recommended Reading

Poet Cursed
Elizabeth Kemball

Callie is born in August; air damp with copper and sweat. Rough hands grab her rust-dipped limbs.

"Why isn't it crying?" Father whispers.

"Open its mouth." Round nurse barks to hawk-nosed nurse.

"When do I get to hold her?" Mother breathes, curling swollen fists into the crumpled sheets. The gaps between the beep-beep of the heart monitor are shrinking.

A rubber-clad finger pushes against petal soft gums and the child's mouth is prised open. A small torch is directed into the dark. The inhale of breath. Delicate silicone tipped pliers pull it into view.

"Poet cursed." Hawk-nosed nurse proclaims.

"Third this week." Round nurse sighs.

Finally, a cry. Not from the babe. Mother lets the tears fall and Father closes the front door. The sun tries to beat it open for a week.

*

Callie is four months old, quiet in her cot. The house is always quiet now. Before her birth, Mother would hum and Father would chatter. The radio gathers dust on the kitchen cupboard. Callie is instead surrounded by *useful* toys; toys that Mother has been ensured will help with her condition. No words. No noises. Nothing too stimulating. Just soft shapes and beiges. Her tiny hands grip a hollow wooden teether, slippery with her spit.

The lines of Mother's face are changing; the edges of her lips curving down into doggish jowls, the bags under her eyes delicate as lunaria annua seed pods, brows constantly pulling towards the ground. It is as if she has given in to gravity. She reaches for one of the books, displayed spine-to-wall, and tracks a line of text on the well-worn page *'There is no pattern to this affliction, the true curse of the poet is to be unknowable'*. Mother wonders instead if that is just the curse of being human.

*

2

At eighteen-months, Father enrols Callie into a specialist nursery; he has to check with his wife on the child's height, weight and eye colour when filling in the forms. Mother insists whilst pouring the morning coffee, that as the girl can't speak, she isn't ready. Still clings to the hope that this is all a mistake; curable not cursed. Father says the idea of Callie speaking makes him sick.

The nursery thrives on keeping children to themselves, designated pods to avoid the afflicted from mixing too much. Specially trained carers. Preliminary studies have shown too much exposure to others ailed with the curse only encourages the rapidness of its progression (or so is claimed by the newspapers Father reads). Studies on the curse are hard for Mother to find and read.

The room is white and clean-lined. One of the tenets: no nursery rhymes. Callie's bramble of umber curls are a fracture in the light room. Two grey-green eyes, too wide, too watchful, try to decipher this new place. Callie is quieter than the other children. She hears them hum, too young to understand the rhythmic pulse of poems that flow through their nonsense sounds. She lines the toys against the floor. Three – Four – Three – Four. Five – Seven – Five. It is a while before she understands what this means.

*

At five, Callie escapes after school into Mother's dressing room, away from the silence of the living room. She climbs onto the quilted stool. It's a deep red, and soft under her fingers. She looks into the gilt-framed mirror; the only one in the house that she is aware of. Leaning forward, breath fogging the glass, she sticks out her tongue and counts three black marks. Each one like ink bleeding into too-thin paper.

> "This is what Father hates,
> little dots – one – two – three.
> These are what resonate
> with all these words inside of me"

*

It is a crisp September day. The doctor's office is cold, and Callie hides her hands inside the arms of her green cardigan. She tries not to think too much about the colour green, it makes her want to sing.

"So, she was seven last month. Just another annual check-up I presume?" The doctor has a soft voice that matches his soft face. Gentle lines that curve from his nostrils to his lips. Crinkles like old newspaper around his eyes. His skin reminds Callie of tree bark, and she wants to tell him but bites her the inside of her cheek until she tastes metal.

"Yes." Mother answers. She says it like her tongue is a lemon – sharp and sour.

"Any issues this year?" The doctor speaks whilst reading the notes on his computer screen. There is a slight frown puckering his brow that doesn't fit his face quite right.

"Well," Mother pauses and looks at Callie the way she usually does these days, with squinted eyes and pursed lips. "She's talking much more than she used to. If you can call it talking. Poeting, lying, or whatever word you want to use. Gibberish really..."

Callie has noticed over the years how Mother and Father's voices have become one – two mouths of a disjointed body. The same intonations, rhythms, words. All bitter and wrong.

"It is talking." The doctor cuts in, his voice slightly louder than before. "I'm sure you know this condition is nothing to worry about. It runs through the maternal line. I saw in your notes Callie that your grandfather passed this down. There are no adverse health effects that we're currently aware of associated with marked individuals…"

"What about the heart issues?" Mother bites.

"A few preliminary studies have found that there may be a link between takotsubo cardiomyopathy – or what you've probably heard called Broken Heart Syndrome – and marked individuals. But as I say these are preliminary and not at all definitive."

"And what of her learning needs? She's already had to join the cursed classes in her school."

"We try not to use the word cursed. It is not medical."

Mother appears not to have heard this and taps her fingers against the black leather bag on her lap. Callie is swinging her legs;

she hates when Mother speaks as if she isn't there. The doctor turns his warm brown gaze to the little girl.

"Callie, how's school going?"

She looks up at Mother.

"Go on, answer him. Don't ramble." A bullet of Mother's spit flies from her barred teeth onto Callie's cheek.

> "I love the classroom,
> the thoughts and words
> that float around
> begging to be heard."

Callie can feel the fluttering of more verses inside her wanting to escape. She swallows them down as the doctor smiles.

"Most parents would be lucky to have a child this devoted to school."

"And after, what do we do with her then?"

The doctor frowns. This is not his job, to unteach the miseducated. He finds that more and more of his time is spent trying to reinform from the misinformation online.

"It's actually been found that there are many skills the marked excel in more than the unmarked individual. They advance quicker in vocabulary, writing, reading. Also, music, dance, art. Outside of the arts there are careers that require high levels of empathy such as carers and counsellors. Also, marketing, media and more. Being marked doesn't close off paths, just changes those that you may have planned for her to follow."

"And what about marrying? Children?"

"Doctors are not experts on everything. Love included. But marked individuals can *and do* have successful relationships. Surely, your own father can attest to that."

When the woman and her quiet daughter leave his office, the doctor looks at the photo of his wife, sitting in the wooden frame on the desk. He remembers the first night they met, dancing, how she had soliloquised his smile. How her words had made his smile widen. How they still bought that tug to his lips each day.

*

"Your grandfather is dying." Mother's voice breaks into the quiet of Callie's bedroom, her tone as detached as if she were announcing dinner were ready.

Since Callie's thirteenth birthday she had spent most of her evenings in her room listening to audiobooks. Mother and Father couldn't stand the sight of her reading novels or poetry collections. Her room was painted a soft caramel and lacked the usual décor of a teenager. Other than her tightly made bed, her room contained a tall white wardrobe, a desk covered in schoolwork, an orderly shelf of textbooks, and a few stuffed animals that she'd outgrown. Callie never brought her friend's home, worried they'd shrivel of boredom in this beige kingdom.

> "Your father? Grandfather mine?
> Whose tongue dripped blackness
> into our bloodline?"

Mother had tried to drown out the sound of Callie's *poems*, even as this one reddened her cheeks.

Callie often wondered about the grandfather her parents never let her meet. Well, not since she could speak. She knew from a doctor's visit long ago that he was the carrier of the mark. Knew that he must have lived for decades, and spoke poetry, and worked, and presumably loved to have created Mother, despite her coldness. Callie tied the laces on her trainers and pulled on her winter coat, almost left the room before her eyes snagged on a small notebook. Poetry class. Mandatory for the marked and unmarked alike – considered a language now. She slipped it deep into her pocket.

Her Grandfather's home is not what she'd imagined. Not that she had visited a care home before. But, despite the name, the books she'd read made her think of a clinical, hospital-like building. *Apollo House* sits a little way out of the city; an old red-brick building surrounded by untrimmed hedges and patches of wildflowers. As her mother pulls the doorbell on the large yellow door, Callie tugs nervously at her sleeves. She is not sure what to say to a dying man. Worse, she worries about those verses pouring out in front of Mother, who stands stiffly next to her, face as impassive as the stone fox that guards the entryway.

"Welcome, welcome,
Lady one, Lady two,
Apollo House,
is open to you."

The rotund woman who opens the door wears a paint splattered apron and has pulled her long, ginger hair into a nest upon her head. Her face is full and broken open with a wonky-toothed smile. She wears a glittery name badge that reads 'Rachael'. Callie likes her instantly.

"We're here to see my father. Alfred Dusk." Mother's voice is crisp.

"Alfie's daughter? I see. I see.
Though not like him, not like me.
No matter, no matter, come on through,
I believe he's waiting for you."

Rachael must have chosen to continue her life with this level of rhyme, letting poems slip out uninhibited. In lessons for the marked, they practised ways to twist their verses into something that resembled plain speech. Callie found herself inexplicably jealous, even though she doesn't really love rhyme anyway.

As Rachael leads them through the corridors towards Grandfather's room, Callie's eyes wander over the walls. There are bright murals littered with words, handwritten poems sprawling over posters, and shelves upon shelves crammed with dog eared books. She knew that people like her existed outside of beige and regime. Knowing and seeing, however, are two separate things.

Down the last corridor, a large window looks out onto the courtyard. Amongst the potted plants growing wild beyond their constraints, a grey-haired man dances with a blue-haired lady. Rachael slows as she follows her gaze

"Sixty-one years of Sammy and Clove,
Love beyond what most will know,
Her tongue a garden to the black,
Not his, but back and forth they flow,
With words and rhymes and joy and warmth,

I see, it sets your heart aglow."

Callie looks up at Rachael and, noticing Mother has wandered down the corridor out of earshot, lets the discipline tying her tongue loosen.

> "Though fragile as dew dampened petals,
> Though rare as an unread bookshelf,
> I want to escape all the blandness
> I want some of that for myself."

Rachael reaches out and squeezes Callie's shoulder.

> "I see some of Alfie in you.
> Do try to have a moment alone,
> He's in room two-three-two,
> Let him tell you his life, little one."

Grandfather's room is painted a wash of blues and greens, seemingly blended at random. He lies on a large bed, afloat in a mess of blankets and throws. His face has the chalky purple tinge of the dying and Callie has to take a few deep breaths before she can step closer. Watery blue eyes track her, and a small smile tugs at the grooves around his lips. The grooves of a poem written over many years of smiling.

> "My daughter, My granddaughter,
> Nothing alike.
> See the tree out my window
> It grew a disease, hidden and toxic
> Under the leaves, and now
> I am dying. It is too.
> Thank you for coming
> Though there's nothing happy I can offer you."

Mother looks different to how Callie has seen her before, her usual straight spine is slumped slightly, and she is picking at her cardigan buttons.

"Dad. How're you?" Her voice is slightly higher than usual, and Callie can see the wave of her throat undulating with each swallow.

> "Dying, darling, but that's okay,
> It was always going to happen one day."

Mother nods curtly and takes Callie's arm more gently than usual to pull her closer to the bed.
"Callie has grown a lot since you last saw her."
Grandfather nods now and for a split-second Callie sees the resemblance between the adults in front of her.

> "Tea, please, Hattie,
> One for you, one for me."

"Okay," Mother whispers. Callie has never heard her voice so quiet. They look at each other and it is so still for a second that she can hear the wind whistle by the window. Then Mother leaves.

Callie tries to think of what to say to this man in front of her; for once the words won't flow at all. Grandfather reaches out and grasps her clammy hand in his papery one. He smells like lemons and honey.

> "Hello, little bird, oh I can see,
> The magic in you has grown from me.
> I can see the feathers right there on your back
> One day, soon, you will fly. Please don't lose track
> Of that feeling you feel right inside you, right there…"

He taps his Adam's apple with one shaky finger.

> "It's the stuff that keeps the world caring,
> and sharing, and knowing, and growing, and breathing.
> Curses are magic, and not all are dark,
> Remember, little bird, you're a marvel, a spark."

His voice trails off at the end and heavy coughing racks his body. Callie's eyes prickle, and when their eyes meet, she lets the tears and her words fall out in a rush.

> "I wish she had let me know you,
> there's so much I want to hear:
> your life, your advice, your poems
> this curse, how you live with it,
> grow with it, know it and twist it…"

Grandfather lifts his finger and presses it gently to Callie's lips. For years to come she could conjure the pressure of that love against her skin.

> "Stop, little bird. I will speak as plainly as I can
> For the truth is, the greatest poem of them all,
> Will always be yourself,
> For you hold no more and no less,
> Than the moon in your mouth,
> And the sun on your breath."

He reaches out then and pats her pocket, the weight of her poetry book pushes against her side. Mother enters, with a tray laden with three cups of tea, and a nurse wearing duck-egg scrubs. They speak about the treatments grandfather has undergone and the pressure currently growing in his lungs. He sits quietly, still holding Callie's hand, only interrupting once to ask for more tea. They don't stay long and as they leave, each of them speaks the one poem known to all. Even Mother.

> "I love you."

*

When the car rumbles slowly off the crunching gravel drive, Callie takes the little black book from her pocket and writes it all down. It starts with a blank page, and the soft etching of *Callie is born in August* staining the silence. Soon, she reaches the words Grandfather said. The colour of the flowers. The dancers in the breeze. She does not stop until her fingers are cramped and smudged with ink. Not once does she look up to see Mother's sharp gaze darting her way.

Grandfather dies three days later. The family attend the funeral but do not read. Rachael sits near the front, in a green dress dotted with forget-me-nots, she waves at them as they take their seats. Callie is glad to see the pews full, and a ceremony bursting with flowers and poetry and music, even though they get up and go with the hymn's last note still ringing in their ears.

*

Callie is eighteen and her long legs are cramped awkwardly around the luggage at her feet. The train smells of coffee and stale breath. Yet, she is smiling. It is a rare sight, just a small curve of her chapped lips, no teeth. There is a judder of the carriage, and she leans down to adjust the tote bag full of fresh books threatening to spill out. Her fingers linger, tracing the words on the spine of the smallest book *Literary Theory: A Very Short Introduction*. A bubble of a giggle escapes her lips, and she doesn't try to swallow it down. University is only six stops away.

She looks out of the window, watching the green fields whir past. Her heart sings at the colour and her hand travels to pat the little black book in her inside pocket. There is a child a few seats down singing nursery rhymes and Callie hums along, so quiet nobody else can hear.

Callie leans her forehead against the cold glass, closes her eyes, and dreams.

The Queue and I
Sally Filer

Signs surround us. Auguries and coincidences, evolving images in clouds, susurrating trees, yet most people seem unaware. Even dreams of future memories are instantly forgotten except for the occasional déja-vu.

I stopped sharing it all when Meg started primary school. Her friends were making fun of her, for having such a weird big sister, and Mum and Dad said I had to stop saying such things, or I'd be locked up. My gift, a family embarrassment, and my insights and interpretations were just perceived as 'Elizabeth's fertile imagination.' I had to keep the ethereal people vying for attention to myself. Mum called them my 'imaginary friends'.

*

Meg is getting married next spring and is therefore no longer a problem. At thirty-four, and going through a divorce, I still am. Meg and I are the same height, slim build, and pale with wild red curly hair; our inheritance from Mum. She had played the part of Queen Elizabeth I, in a school play, and subsequently considered herself royal. We used to curtsy when she wore her hair up, with a high-necked pie-crust blouse, imagining she resembled the young Princess Diana. However, her new Avon translucent face-powder made her more the image of Miranda Richardson's Elizabeth I, in Dad's favourite - *Blackadder*. We shortened our names from Elizabeth and Margaret as soon as we were old enough to realise. Meg, of course, has now become more acceptable after Prince Harry's wedding, but whenever anyone asks about Lizzie, Mum looks confused and mutters, "Oh, you must mean my Elizabeth."

*

The morning after my shotgun marriage to Ed I knew I'd made a mistake. It's difficult to find peace when your future constantly invades the present and limitations loomed before me. Perhaps there is only peace in the past because we know what happened, good or bad. Mum and Dad thought Ed was perfect. Meg didn't. When I lost the baby, Ed and I swung between intimacy and antagonism before agreeing on a no-fault divorce. I immediately cut my hair short and dyed it black to become someone else, but it didn't work. Mum said I just looked terminally ill. It's red and unruly again now. Only the pythoness tattoo coiling up my arm remains.

*

Meg, Mum, and I left home at 5:15 this morning to begin a 'once-in-a-lifetime experience,' as Mum insists on describing it. Our modern-day pilgrimage to view a coffin guarded by soldiers in heavy uniforms, from past centuries, draped with the Royal Standard. My father, who leaves the room every Christmas afternoon as soon as the first image of Windsor Castle appears on TV, told us we were 'bloody mad' and declined to join us.

Mum argued,"It'll do us all good, John, to get out of this house and focus on something else."

Being partial to purple velvet, Mum has worn her hat and matching scarf for the occasion and is unimpressed by our Nike's, Puffa jackets and jeggings. The train into London is packed and stuffy, but we find Mum a seat, while Meg and I stand swaying, air-pods tuned to Radiohead.

As we descend into Bank, the deepest and most confusing of tube stations, a warm, dusty and suffocating wind creates a cacophony of coughing.

Gripping her scarf over her mouth, Mum shouts, "Well, they've soon forgotten the coronavirus!"

We blend into the confused crowd, veering in every direction, like ants, in search of the right exit, while dodging sleeping homeless people. On finally emerging at Southwark we are greeted by a cobalt sky and shouting marshals in high-vis vests and lanyards. They direct us, like air hostesses, towards water fountains, first-aid stations, portaloos and the end of the queue, before distributing green paper wristbands to indicate our position. We are informed we currently have a fourteen-hour wait.

Mum, who expected the queue to be mainly middle-England, John Lewis customers, keeps looking around and commenting loudly on 'diversity,' her new word. Initially, it feels exciting to be part of such a historic event, though the atmosphere is mixed. Some appear grief-stricken and tearful, as if a member of their own family has died, while others laugh, enjoying themselves. Many still wear masks despite being outside, though the air can hardly be called fresh; glinting white aeroplanes from Heathrow crisscross above, while throbbing red buses, black taxis and white vans emit a continual shimmer of pollutants. The CNN news reporter nearby describes the queue as, 'an embodiment of the national mood, a symbolic ritual to be undertaken.' They obviously haven't spoken to Dad.

*

After the first few hours spent shuffling forward and taking the usual photos of landmarks, I start to feel the others vying for my attention. Their communication is usually gentle - a slight vibration on my left side before materialising on my right. They're faint, like an imprint, and sometimes I only hear a voice. I've disciplined myself to appear normal and unflustered, during sudden visitations, to avoid any suspicion from Mum. Meg knows it happens but insists I don't tell her. It terrifies her and then she can't sleep.

As we pass Victoria Tower Gardens a flock of crows, cawing above the bronze statue of Emmeline Pankhurst, alert me before the vibration. She materialises wearing an elegant navy coat, brown fur collar, pearls and a high feathered hat. I feel like a peasant. She points ahead, looking towards Big Ben, before whispering in a cut-glass accent,

"In the early 20th century, I was held in a secret prison cell within the tower of Big Ben - it was used for troublemakers within the palace."

She places an ethereal gloved hand on my arm.

"You, Elizabeth, must continue the fight."

Her violet eyes are insistent.

"Many women still suffer terribly."

As she dissolves, I take a few breaths to ground myself. She has made me feel nostalgic. How did I lose Lizzie, the ardent feminist at Uni, marching and campaigning? Can I really just blame Ed and the pregnancy? I hesitate for a while, but as we pass Big Ben it's too interesting not to share, though I omit her presence and personal message.

Mum looks impressed, "I hadn't realised you'd learned so much history doing that English degree."

Then adds, under her breath, "In the two years before you dropped out."

Meg winks, "Fancy a stroll - get some coffee?"

Mum intervenes, "No, you stay here with the bags. I'll go with Margaret; I need to find a loo."

*

I continue the shuffle forward, tuning in to centuries-old oaks and beeches, but as we approach Tate Britain, I detect a musty smell and a faint wailing. A painfully thin woman, initially dappled and insubstantial in the sunlight, materialises dressed in brown-stained rags and wearing rusty handcuffs. When she is sure of my full attention, she swings around pointing to the area behind her.

"See all this?"

I nod.

"Originally, it was seven acres of marshland and the infamous Millbank penitentiary."

Her accent is cockney and guttural.

"We weren't allowed to speak, detained in silence, under Mr Bentham's, 'panopticon principle' experiment, before crossing over from the prison passageway to barges moored on the Thames. To be transported!" She blinks compulsively. "My life was brief and terrible, and I died at sea before reaching Australia. Elizabeth, you must use your gift and live before it's too late!"

I make a mental note to google Jeremy Bentham while watching her disintegrate and attempt to focus on the present. I concentrate on the two women pushing a buggy laden with bags in front. My legs are starting to ache, and I envy the sleeping toddler cosily wrapped in the pushchair. As the woman with a blonde plait turns to glance down at him I realise she's pregnant. I never really noticed pregnant women, but now I see them everywhere, signifying success – they had managed to keep their babies. Initially, I was mortified when I realised I was pregnant and my first thought was not to keep it, but Ed was ecstatic, and I was swept along with his emotion, and Mum's enthusiasm for her first grandchild. The grief is a shock, I never expected to feel this bereft, and still retain a residual sense of guilt at my body's incompetence. I eavesdrop on their conversation in an attempt to change the 'grief' channel. The mother of the toddler says the most relaxation she has had in two years was during a recent MRI. Her friend empathises, saying her husband spends so little time at home she thinks he must have a secret second family.

    Mum and Meg eventually return with dire warnings about the state of the portaloos. I follow the yellow arrows and spot them, incongruously positioned, in front of a gleaming white 900-year-old church - St Margaret's. A long snaking queue has formed in front of each loo and I start fishing in my bag for tissues. I detect a faint vibration, and think I must be imagining it, but as I look up an impatient-looking Winston Churchill, wearing a top hat and tails, is at my side. He points out a roman boundary stone embedded in the churchyard near my left foot before admiring St Margaret's.

    "I was married to Clementine in this church in 1908."

    I glance up at its white spire piercing the now perfect ultramarine sky. When I look back at him, he's smiling.

    "We were married for fifty years and had five children."

    He carefully considers me before adding, "You too will marry again, and have children."

    As he slowly disintegrates I experience a strange, floating, disembodied sensation. I'm used to the permeability of my inner and outer boundaries, but this particular combination of the present, the past and talk of the future is new. He said, "children?"

    I amble back to find Mum and Meg chatting with a lively Scottish family. Meg to the glamorous couple with twins and Mum to a woman with a florid face, and her vicar husband. He seems to be living his best life preaching to a captive audience, while his wife looks bored and irritated.

    He nods repeatedly,

    "Yes, yes, the past couple of years with coronavirus lockdowns do seem like a strange time warp."

    Mum introduces me and I immediately forget all their names. An awkward silence follows. Mum fills it,

    "Well, how lucky was Liz Truss, our new prime minister, getting to meet the Queen at Balmoral, just days before she died?"

The vicar closes his eyes and nods.

"This moment we share is a rupture in time, the loss of our queen, the new prime minister, and now a new King to usher in the 'Carolean age'."

He glances at his wife.

"I believe it has been named?"

She forces a smile.

"Yes, dear, it has."

Mum smiles and points ahead,

"Look at all the cameras and news readers girls, we might be on TV!"

The vicar continues, "We are all part of an extraordinary event, extraordinary! All these selfless people showing their respect for our monarch of seventy years. Such an uplifting contrast to the evil of Putin's evil war in the Ukraine."

Meg immediately begins an urgent discussion with me about options for her wedding bouquet on her phone, to prevent the imminent sermon, while we agree via WhatsApp on the hot male half of the glamorous couple, but neither of us can remember his name.

A strong vibration compels me to look behind. Elizabeth the second, our late Queen, is meandering through the pilgrims towards me surrounded by flickers and flashes of bright light. She stops and scrutinises me for a few seconds. I feel myself redden before stumbling into something resembling a curtsy.

She confides, "All these conversations about me are enormously fascinating, though one does feel rather guilty - not actually being in the coffin. A terrorist attack, you see, or Mr Putin pushing the dreaded button, my remains may have flailed out along the mall, and of course, we couldn't have that. Everyone seems to have accepted I am there - I suppose that's all that matters. Death is utter bliss by the way. The peace that passeth all understanding. Finally, anonymity! The irony - if only everyone knew."

Archangel Michael, who had been keeping watch from the entrance of Shakespeare's Globe, beckons her across. As she draws near to him, his iridescent wings refract her lights and send cascades of rainbow-colours ricocheting across the Thames.

Meg snaps, "Stop practising your curtsy, everyone's looking, and why ARE you smiling? We've still got at least another seven hours of this, and anyway, I'm not actually sure you're supposed to curtsy at her coffin!"

*

Hours later, as we inch closer to Westminster Hall, we feel briefly excited, but it's an anti-climax - the queue transforms into an even longer snaking zigzag. To escape Mum's constant interference in her wedding plans Meg starts chatting again with the couple behind and calls me over.

"Guess what? Andy went to the same Uni as you."

He smiles at me, he has the bluest of eyes, I feel myself redden and manage to stutter, "Oh, really, what did you study, I - I mean, read?"

He grimaces, "Mathematics, but what my sister didn't tell Meg, is that I dropped out before my final exams."

His sister.

I smile, "So did I, I meant to go back after a year, but then I didn't."

We connect instantly and while ostensibly sharing modules, societies, and friends we find ourselves flirting. Meg winks at me, while suggesting to his sister, Lauren, that they should take their niece and nephew to look for swans on the Thames. Andy smiles and explains that after moving to London and trying various lines of work he's now decided to study medicine at Cambridge. He credits his father for inspiring him, with a quote from Ralph Ellison,

"The end is in the beginning and lies far ahead."

He said, "It felt like he'd given me permission, you know, to start again."

Meanwhile, Mum and the vicar's wife are engrossed in a whispered conversation about Olivia Coleman's portrayal of the Queen, in *The Crown*, compared to her Queen Anne, in *The Favourite* - arms are folded and eyebrows are raised. When Meg, Lauren and the twins finally return Andy, and I are in hysterics, as if we'd always known each other.

*

As dusk arrives one of the twins is sick and has a suspicious itchy rash. Andy and his family reluctantly decide to abandon the queue and we all say our goodbyes. I wish I could go with them, the three of us are tetchy, cold and achingly tired.

We trudge towards the entrance of Westminster Hall in the dark. It's significantly colder. The queue falls silent as we halt, temporarily, on the marble stairs before the descent to the catafalque. Communal grief is catching, and many are clutching tissues, even my stomach churns. After hours of anticipation we are finally looking up at her coffin. Mum is tearful, gripping our hands, and we clumsily curtsy together. This surreal moment will be etched in my memory forever.

*

As we emerge everyone looks lost in a trance of their own, like guests at a party that had gone on too long. Meg checks google maps for the nearest tube, while I find myself staring at a nearby squirrel, frozen like a question mark. I feel a faint vibration as we start heading away, but resist. I'm far too tired, however, this one doesn't materialise.

He just whispers, "I, Oliver Cromwell, was declared Lord Protector in this hall in 1653. After my death, my decomposing head was stuck on the roof where it stayed for twenty-five years until being blown down by a storm. I was relieved in 1960 when it was finally buried in my old Cambridge college chapel."

His tone changes, "I envisage you, Elizabeth, at Cambridge."

*

When we eventually arrive home, drained and exhausted, a variety of dusty cardboard boxes are cluttering the hall. Mum starts tutting at the mess.

"What on earth? John? I don't believe it; he's had all bloody day. John!"

A dusty-looking Dad emerges from the sitting room and hugs me.

"I've been thinking about you, Elizabeth."
"Really? Why?"

"Well, your mother left her usual list so I thought I'd better make a start with bringing the cases down from the attic, but I couldn't get the damn ladder down. It was those boxes from granny's I'd shoved up there last year when we finished clearing out the last of her stuff. I made the mistake of opening one and I've been engrossed for hours - all those old black-and-white photos! Been sitting here racking my brain, trying to remember who they all were. I was about to pile them all back in the boxes, before you came back, when I spotted this battered old notebook lying at the bottom of one."

He hands me a worn, stained, faded, brown diary smelling of mildew. It feels like it could crumble in my hand.

"I think you might follow your great, great-grandmother, Alexandra."

"Do I?"

"It's fascinating, pages of herbal remedies in miniscule writing. I had to get your mother's magnifying glass to read it - she's even drawn tiny herbs on each page. At the back, there's a faint drawing of a snake next to some poem. She mentions seeing the future in clouds and there's something about being called a witch - communing with spirits."

Meg widens her eyes.

"Oh wow, let's see!"

She squints to read.

> 'Fold above fold a surging maze, his head
> Crested aloft and carbuncle his eyes;
> With burnished neck of verdant gold, erect
> Amidst his circling spires, that on the grass
> Floated redundant; pleasing was his shape,
> And lovely.'

I slump back into the armchair. I remember studying Milton and *Paradise Lost*, and experiencing a deep connection with it. It was the only essay I managed to achieve a first in.

A familiar, pungent, herby odour makes its presence felt before Alexandra whispers, "Remember the primordial coils of the insinuating serpent in the Paradise garden - go back to University, complete your studies and write. All will be well."

I've been aware of this odour when feeling lost and alone, but she's never communicated before. Mum bustles in with mugs of tea looking exasperated.

"I've been listening, what nonsense, your great-grandmother was nothing like our Elizabeth, John. Your mother always said Alexandra was mad - they even had to have her sectioned a few times! Don't you go telling our Elizabeth she's like her. Pay no attention to him, girls."

Dad looks deflated.

Mum changes the subject, "And, anyway, don't you want to hear about our day?"

Meg relates the events of the day before Mum interrupts, "Go on, tell him, Elizabeth."

"Well, I think I've decided to go back to university."

"And?" Mum's smiling, "What else?"

"I've been asked out by a hot Scotsman."

Meg adds, "Who is only training to be a doctor!"

Mum interrupts, "Shame he's called Andrew, but then you can't have everything."

Unwoven
Bethany Lewis

Once, it had felt like silk in her hands. Thea had spent the best part of three years letting weft threads glide between her fingers with a soft tickle, weaving them in and out of the loom like quill to paper. But what once was silk now scorched her skin like flame, forming new fingerprints.

Of course, she was not supposed to be the weaver for the court. As Queen Lyra's sister, Thea's place in the castle was unquestionable. But Lyra had insisted, and so, when Thea came of age, she became the one to document the history of their people into small tapestry squares like the weavers before her. She could not help feeling pride well within her each time a new square was completed.

Sat on the floor of her dark chambers, Thea rolled her eyes at how quickly that heart-felt pride had twisted into a small knot of string in her stomach, that became larger and more tangled every time she dared look at the two tapestries on the loom above her. She pulled them toward her once more. Neither were complete, and only one could be the final square, the tapestry that would complete the story of Lyra's reign.

The knot was going to constrict her organs. It was going to close off her throat from the inside and would not stop until it spun around her heart. *But*, Thea thought, staring at the blood on her hands. It had pooled on her palms and ran down her arms in thin, intertwining lines.

Maybe that's for the best.

It was almost quiet, except for the crackling of the embers in the hearth. The town just outside the castle would still be asleep, the night's horrors would not disturb their dreams. Thea envied them. Envied the way Lyra's advisors would ensure that no news about their queen's death would reach them. Hours ago, she knew that was best, but now, she wasn't sure of anything.

The burning village.
No.

Thea forced her eyes shut and clenched her fists around the bottom of her *peplos*, trying to allow her thoughts to drift. Lyra always told her to steady her breathing in these moments, but Thea could not. With every pop and every crack of the fire, she saw a flash of the cloaked killer, the dagger, Lyra falling to her side. With the dying embers Thea saw the people, others she would rather forget. Instead, she leaned against the wall and forced herself to look at what was in front of her. Bed. Table. Clepsydra. Loom.

She was grateful that the castle was warm. Even during unrelenting winters, Lyra ensured every hearth had enough flint and wood for constant fires, and the court had the thickest fabrics in the doorways to block out the cold. Even when they were children and the castle was less prepared for winter, Lyra would ensure Thea slept on the bed closest to their fire and insisted that she curled up under the biggest wolfskin quilt.

Thea wiped her eyes. She had found her sister, almost lifeless, failing to cover the blood that seeped alarmingly from the wound in her stomach. It pooled in her mouth and dripped onto Thea's shaking hands.

"The window. I saw her in the mirror. The dagger. The spiralled hand."

Thea shuddered. Lyra had been barely audible when she spoke, as quiet as snowfall. She shook herself out of the memory and stared at the first tapestry, *Lyra's tapestry*. She had weaved Lyra lying in the centre, blood collecting at her waist, her crown fallen by her side. She had weaved the hand of her sister's killer in the corner, holding a dagger, stained scarlet.

This tapestry. *Lyra's tapestry* was correct. She would unveil it at the ceremony tomorrow. Thea pulled the second tapestry, which she had taken to calling *Iris' tapestry,* from the loom without looking at it, and rolled it into her pouch out of sight. It was a slight on her sister's memory. Outside, the leaves moved slowly in the wind, and Thea tried to match her breathing to their back-and-forth movements. Directly below her chambers were the cages, and Thea imagined the cloaked killer, Iris, trying to do the same. She clutched *Lyra's tapestry* in her hands.

Good.

There was a creak behind her, a shuffling at the end of the corridor. Thea jumped, turning to face the door, the tapestry squeezed underneath her fingers turning her knuckles white. It was far too early for Cyril to collect *Lyra's tapestry*. Without thinking,

Thea balled it up and stuffed it into her pouch. She held her breath as the footsteps approached the door, the tapestry pouch growing heavier in her hands.

The footsteps passed her door, without a knock, and Thea closed her eyes in relief. She dumped the pouch on the ground and sank next to it. Her stomach rippled, pushing its knots against the surface. She pulled out both tapestries. If it was *Lyra's tapestry* she had chosen, then she should finish it, go to Cyril herself, and throw the other tapestry in the fire. Thea faced the flames, *Iris's tapestry* balled in her fist. She took a deep breath and inhaled a thick smoke that clogged her senses.

It was no use. Thea threw *Iris's tapestry* aside in frustration and picked at the mud on the bottom of her dress, ignoring the footprint stamped onto the back of her hand. There was no point thinking about that now, and she willed herself to be rid of it. Cyril, her sister's head advisor, with his twinkling eyes and looming stature, had told her as much. Cyril only told you something once.

She wished she hadn't gone out there. If she hadn't, then she would have handed Cyril the completed tapestry. Then her nephew, Dion, would be crowned king. When Dion was king, Lyra could be avenged, and Thea would weave. Thea stared at the dancing tapestries on the wall, hoping the drip, drip, drip of the clepsydra would drown out the noises jumping around her head. It did not. She needed to choose and choose correctly. Thea leaned against the wall once more. If she re-lived it, she would know. Eyes closed; Thea cast her mind back once again.

*

It had just turned midnight. Thea had twisted her shuttle, letting the weft threads tangle in between her fingers. The wailing from the other end of the hall had informed her that Dion knew of his mother's death. Thea clutched her shuttle. Dion's nursemaids would console him, but she had work to do. The boy continued to cry. At just nine years old, he had never known death. Thea untangled the weft threads and tightened them to the shuttle. He would thank her when he was older.

The tapestry was almost complete. There was just one part left to weave, but Thea did not know where to begin.

"Her dagger-wielding hand. A circle of spirals."

That was all Lyra had told her. It should have been enough, but Thea hesitated. There could be no uncertainty as to who was responsible for this. No one in the towns left wondering, questioning. Not a moment's doubt that Iris should go unpunished. Thea needed to be sure. She draped her cloak around her shoulders. There was only one way to know.

No one looked at her as she ran through the castle. Thea passed the statues of the gods on the stairs. Moved beyond the point where the plush carpet ended, and the floor grew uneven and damp. She went further down still, and the air nipped at her face. She could see her breath lingering in the open like will o' wisps. The cages were cesspits of rot, and urine, and blood. Many of them were full, cluttered with the dead and the living. Weak hands reached out as Thea passed. Many opened their mouths, but no sound came out.

Thea spotted her alone in the last cage, hugging her knees. She faltered, seeing the blood covering Iris's hands. She almost turned back, but she thought of Lyra lying on the ground, crying for her son, and then rattled the cage. Iris looked up. Her face was ashen.

"Come closer." The quiver in Thea's voice betrayed her.

Still, Iris moved closer.

"Give me your hand."

Iris looked at her. Thea couldn't help but notice her gaunt cheekbones, bruised arms and wide eyes. She scowled and reached inside the cage and pulled the woman's hand towards her. A circle of spirals stared back.

"You killed my sister."

The woman bowed her head. her toothless mouth hung open; a foul smell trickled out of it.

"Please. My children." Her voice cracked.

Thea ignored her. She fixed her gaze on the tattoo and traced her fingers across it.

"My children. They're going to kill my children."

Despite herself, Thea looked up.

"Who?"

"The men who left. The man with the twinkling eyes."

The woman reached out and held onto Thea's cloak with a shaking hand.

"Help them. You have to help them. The village at the edge of the wood. *Please.*"

"This is nonsense. An attempt to buy yourself some time before you are punished for your treason."

"We are suffering. My youngest will starve, he-" Iris paused and held a filthy hand to her heart. The seams of her frock were fraying, and Thea could see the prominence of her ribcage. "You take it all and leave us with nothing."

"Everyone must give coin. It is the tithe. It is the law."

"This is more than tithe. Please, you have to save my children. The guards, they-"

"Enough."

Thea continued to stare at the tattoo as Iris wept. When she was sure it was burned into her mind's eye, she let go and marched towards the doors.

Then she stopped.

An uncomfortable thought crawled into her head. There were no guards. There were always guards in the cages. Her heartbeat quickened, and as she left the room she turned not to the stairs, but to the stables.

She was unsure how long she had been travelling. She had never made any visits to the outer villages, except when she was very small. That responsibility fell only to the queen, and Lyra hardly mentioned them.

The sky was filled with thick fog, almost starless. Thea turned to the path behind her. Nothing. It did not feel wise to travel alone at night. Not for the first time, Thea considered turning back, shuddering at the idea of being lost on the road. But she thought of Iris's words and pressed on. There were deep grooves in the path before her, made by wagon wheels. This provided some comfort, at least, that others had also travelled the same way. Thea hoped she would see them on the path, and she would no longer be alone.

There was a faint smell of burning wood. As Thea rode forward, it became stronger, and her eyes began to stream. She realised she was no longer breathing through the fog but breathing in a thick, invasive smoke that made her heave with heavy breaths. Worse still was the screaming. It was distant at first, and so quiet Thea mistook it for birds cawing in the trees. But as the smoke became thicker, the screaming became louder. She pushed her horse into a gallop and raced down the hill into the village below.

It was burning.

Smoke billowed from every window and crack in the walls of a small, thatched-roof house. Castle guards and villagers stood outside. Thea spotted two little figures amongst the villagers, huddled together in a holey, sheepskin quilt with a long piece of thread snaking the ground.

The guards pushed the villagers away from the house. Thea could see many of them, bone thin and dirty, huddled together. Some were crying and shaking from the bitter wind. Others shouted protests at the guards, only to be met with the sharp, grating noise of an unsheathed sword. One man with many wrinkles moved past Thea towards the burning building, a water pail clutched between his fingers.

"This is their home! This is all they have! You've locked Iris away to rot. I won't let you burn the home of her children."

He edged closer to the house. A guard thrust his shield, knocking the man to the floor with a thump. He lay unmoving. The village erupted. Before Thea could move, she saw people taking hold whatever they could find. Some threw stones and sticks, while the others dug their hands into the earth and hurled balls of mud at the guards. The fight came directly towards Thea. Her horse reared on its hind legs and bolted.

A hard jolt knocked the wind out of her. Thea gasped, blinking rapidly as the raucous swarm of people and fire whirled around her. A set of footsteps raced past her, and Thea felt the pinch of a shoe pressing her hand deeper into the mud.

"Sorry."

The voice was small and tearful. Thea turned around in time to see a thin, pale child running, dragging another along with a tiny fist. The old sheepskin quilt lay abandoned at her feet.

"Wait!" Thea scrambled to her feet; their quilt bundled in her arms. They were gone.

Thea whirled around directionless, dodging crowds as she ran into the smoke. She ran into a clearing at the edge of the village, and spotted a stable nestled in between trees. Breathing heavily, Thea trudged towards it, clutching the quilt to her chest. She heard faint whispering inside.

"Miss Thea."

Her head snapped to the side. His stature loomed over her. Cyril always had a presence surrounding him. In court, his voice rang through her ears like silk, always finding a way to lull the others from their heated discussions. He had been Lyra's head advisor for many years, which showed in the curved wrinkles surrounding his twinkling eyes.

"Cyril."

"You have ventured far from the castle."

"I-"

Thea could not speak. She latched onto Cyril's shoulder, wheezing out smoke.

"It does not matter. We will take you home."

Thea frowned.

"Why is this happening?"

She looked at the village surrounding her. The wind had carried the flames beyond the burning house, and it seemed as though the whole village was alight.

"They burned her house."

Even in the heavy smoke, Cyril's eyes still twinkled.

"Yes, Thea."

"Because she killed Lyra?"

"Yes, Thea."

Thea's hands were shaking. She wrapped herself in the holey, sheepskin quilt.

"Cyril. I don't understand. There are children here. These people, they didn't do anything. Lyra wouldn't want this. We need to stop this now."

Just behind her, Thea heard wheels turning in the dirt. There were wagons, Thea counted at least ten, travelling through the mud, marking the earth with every turn of the wheel. Her family crest was carved into the side of them. Inside the wagons were several ripped burlap sacks. Thea couldn't see what was inside, but watched with wide eyes as grains, dead livestock, and the odd bronze coin fell at her feet. The wagons passed Thea and travelled out of sight.

A young girl trailed after them. Her dark hair hang limp above her shoulders, and she had several bald spots on her head where it had fallen out in clumps. She screamed, breathless.

"You can't take the crops anymore! We'll starve! We'll-"
A wagon rolled over her foot.
Thea turned to Cyril.
"What is this?"
"The tithe. Food for winter. Clothing for winter. Sheets and rugs and warmth for the winter."
"For who?"
She searched Cyril's bright eyes.
"For you. For us all."
In the distance, Thea heard the quiet cries and screams of villagers. She shook, but not from cold.
"This cannot be tithe. Coin is tithe. Lyra's-"
"Not everyone has coin, Thea. The law is clear."
Thea ignored him. She turned to the wagon behind her. A guard, smaller than the others, guided the wagon forward. Thea recognised him as the one assigned to watch her room at night.
"Stop the cart. Look at these people."
The guard winced and stopped. He fixed his gaze to the floor, and mumbled something Thea didn't catch, before moving forward with heavy footsteps.
Cyril squeezed Thea's shoulder gently.
"If we don't survive, neither do our people. Most of us will. Thanks to your sister."
"But these villagers-Lyra wouldn't do this."
"She has saved us many winters, Thea."
Thea opened her mouth, then closed it again.
Cyril took the old sheepskin from her shoulders and placed it on a nearby cart.
"This cannot happen again. The people are relying on us. Now, come. You have work to finish. We have caught Lyra's assassin, and the young prince is waiting for his crown."

*

She lay on the floor, pulling string in and out of her fingers and twisting it together. Thea willed herself to sit up, but waves of nausea rooted her head to the carpet. She savoured a few more moments in the quiet of her chambers, without having to think. Her mind drifted out of her memory and to Lyra, but her thoughts grew cloudy, filled with smoke. She wiped her eyes and inhaled deeply, pulling cold air and the smell of blood down her throat. She pushed it back into the room, watching the smoke spread into the open and sink into the furniture and walls. She shivered but sat up and finally, reached out to *Iris's tapestry*, and unfolded it.

Thea traced her fingers across the picture. She brushed over Iris, fully weaved into the frame. She was face down with a hand outstretched to a holey, sheepskin quilt she couldn't quite reach. Thea let teary blotches stain the centre of the picture. They fell from her face onto Lyra's, who lay there with a blank expression, in a burning village, her own hand sinking a dagger deep into her heart.

As the sun rose, her loom cast long shadows over her. Cyril would soon knock to collect a tapestry and the ceremony would begin. She would carry it to the hall. Unveil it to the crowd and drape it over Lyra's coffin. All Thea needed to do was finish one.

She stared at *Iris's tapestry*. She could unveil it. Listen to the sounds of the coronation from the cages as they replaced Iris' body with hers. She did not know for how long she would have to watch the wheels of a wagon rolling next to the little cage window.

She stared at *Lyra's tapestry*. She could unveil it. Honour her sister and nephew and stand still at Iris' execution. Stand still at the window of her chambers, watching as the guards weaved the wagons of tithe through the palace grounds, eyes fixed to the floor like statues in motion. She did not know how long she would have to weave for her nephew under Cyril's twinkling eyes.

Someone knocked lightly. The knot in her stomach grew tighter and began to travel up to her throat. Her heart was stuck on a single beat. She clutched both tapestries in her hands as tears blurred her periphery. She had to choose one. Another light knock. Thea's eyes started back and forth between her work, her hands starting to shake. Another light knock. With a mirthless cry, Thea slammed the tapestries to the ground. She tore into them, her nails like talons, ripping and ripping until they were an amalgamation of threads in a heap on the floor.

She exhaled, no longer able to smell blood, or smoke, and she could not hear the rapping at the door. Or if she did, she ignored it, and instead lay down in the heap she had made and let the wind scatter the threads across the wooden floor.

Heaven is a Coffee Shop
Lucy Aur

I never told him I loved him.
But today I will.

Today I will say something like this:

"You can go find a seat; I'll get these." I squeeze my purse in my hand, reassuring myself it's still there and I haven't lost it. There's two people in front of me in the queue; that's enough time to rehearse whatever order he gives me. He looks at me, eyebrows furrowed and pouting.

"Girl, I'm not leaving you." He bumps my shoulder and smiles. "I saw the window seat is free anyway. Don't rush, don't stress."

I smile too. I don't know what I'm going to order, the menu is too long and too small for me to grasp. I want just a cup of tea but there doesn't seem to be *just tea* available. We get to the front, the white-toothed man welcomes us and asks for our order, cup ready in his hand to scribble down a wrong spelling of our names. He has a piercing through his septum, he scrunches his nose as he waits for me to say something

"Vanilla latte with almond milk please, large or whatever you call it."

"Same please," I spit out.

I don't really like caffeine anymore; it makes my head feel heavy. But a heavy head is easier than the sickness I feel trying to pick my own drink. They've got digital menus now and they change too fast for me to even finish reading one item. He looks at me, knowing that is not the drink I wanted. He rolls his eyes and turns back to the smiling man.

"Can we get a pot of tea as well, two cups." We're answered with a smile and a tray as we shuffle our way to the end of the counter. I lean into him, my way of saying *thank you, sorry, you're the best.* His jumper is soft against my cheek, I trace the gold lettering *Gucci* across his chest and laugh.

"What?"

"You're so cool now," I say quietly.

"It was a gift; I'm not spending that money on a jumper, but I will gladly wear it."

"You look good, like always."

"Stop, hun you look gorgeous. This outfit is giving me clueless vibes, love it." He plays with the buckle on my yellow tartan dungarees. I feel my cheeks grow warm as I try my best not to let a wide grin swallow my face. He grabs the tray - nothing clatters and I head towards the stairs. I know better than to offer to carry it. We sit in the window seat, facing each other and ignoring the room. It's early autumn and the sun is bright on his face. The coffee shop smells of cinnamon and his father's cologne. I know it's his father's because he tells me every time. He pulls out his phone.

"Smile!" I do my most basic beam and let him snap away, compliments falling from his lips with every new angle. None of the photos I take of him ever look good enough, he's an oil painting in the flesh. Too full of beauty and life to be stilled into a screen. That being said, his Instagram is a digital Tate gallery in itself.

"Come here." he shuffles up next to me and brings the camera closer to us. I love it when he takes photos of us, especially the ones that never get posted anywhere. The photos remind me of what was real, when the memories start to fade and I forget his voice, I know this photo will bring him back to me.

"I miss you." I look at him, properly. His sharp clenched jaw, his perfectly sprayed hair, how his eyes dart around the room at every noise. Something is different about him, he's taller than I remember, and he slouches. He never slouched before.

"I'm right here," he looks right at me, poking his tongue out.

"You know what I mean."

He turns away from me and picks up his mug. It's still too hot, I can see the steam, but he drinks anyway. He's beautiful even when he's sad.

"Yeah, well you didn't have to bring it up." He still won't look at me. His left leg bounces. He always bounced his left leg. Or was it his right?

"Just stop it." He glares at me.

"Stop what?"

"Thinking these things. It's in your head that these thoughts are made, and in your head, they can be stopped. Get back to the good stuff please." His face softens, almost pleading.

I shake the thoughts from my head, emptying the frustration I feel and scold myself for taking things down this route. I breathe in, I breathe out. I start again,

"I love tea." How boring. Why is that what comes out of my mouth.

"Drinking it or spilling it?" He's smiling again now.

This version of me doesn't appear often, especially recently. I'm saying things I don't normally say with a confidence that I force. I'm sat with my back straight and my legs crossed as I lean into the wall, a typical girl pretending she is more than she is. I'm not that comfortable but I don't know how to be, and I definitely don't have time to be thinking this much about it. I've already wasted enough.

"Have you written anything recently? Catch me up, I miss your stories." He holds my hand, his much softer than mine, as he twists the rings on my finger. I see him looking at them and know that whatever I say now he will not hear. I slide the rings off my fingers and pass them to him, watching the smile on his face grow as he puts them onto his own.

"I'm listening, I swear!"

"I haven't written in months if I'm honest. I don't think I've written anything all year. It's like my hands have mutism."

"Nothing? What about that historical story you were writing, was that the one set in the museum where there's a girl who can talk to the dead famous people? And there was one about the murdered Queen? Or any poetry? You wrote poetry every day I thought," he tilts his head as he looks at me, like he's figuring out a weird Picasso painting.

I remember this moment, the moment sat in the window seat feeling as though the world outside had stopped just for us. I remember thinking about how much I was going to miss it before it was even over. My mind tugs between now and then and I find myself getting everything muddled up.

*

There is a clock on the wall. I hadn't noticed it when we came in. It says it's quarter to four. This place shuts at four in the winter.

"Five. It shuts at five, regardless of the seasons. Unless you're thinking of…" he says.

"No, I'm not, my mistake."

"If you have to go you can, it's fine. Nobody stays as long as you do anyway."

"I stay because I want to."

"Not because you feel bad?"

"Why are you being mean to me?"

"*I'm* not."

I take two large gulps of my cold tea and push the empty cup away from me.

"I have to go now." He says, passing back my rings and sitting up straight. I'm not thinking of things in the right way, and he knows. Well, this version of him knows.

"No." I say. I don't snap, I don't shout, but I say it. "Please stay."

"You know I can't. Our cups are empty, time to go baby."

I always hate when I get to this part. It's the chapter everyone skips in a book, the film scene you leave the room for. I don't have that luxury. I can't escape this moment. I've tried before.

"I'll be up again soon, maybe next month?"

"Doesn't matter when, I'm not going anywhere." He doesn't say this nicely. His jaw is tense, and he won't look at me. I hate when I get to this part.

"I'm sorry."

"It's not your fault." His voice is quieter. I can hear the cars on a nearby road, children's footsteps chasing after a parent, birds and sirens and someone else's conversation. I turn my head away from the noise, trying to remember what we were saying.

He's further away from me now, leaving without saying goodbye again. It's like I'm not there, like nobody is there. The room falls away from me, and it's just him.

"I love you." I whisper. He doesn't hear me. "Hey, I love you." I shout louder but still he's fading away. I shout it loud in the hope that if he can hear me, he'll turn around. As if somehow, I can change what has already happened.

My heart hurts. I feel it in my chest, I feel the pulling, the tugging, and the crushing. I feel the weight of the words I didn't say enough, they clutter up my insides and leave no room for anything new. I stumble over thoughts; I can't recall the ending. I can't picture us hugging goodbye, I can't picture him waving from the bus stop, I can't remember if he texted me to say he got home safe.

The scene jams in my head, it skips forward until there is only static. I flick through other moments, paper cutting myself trying to find one I can force my focus into. I see our first day of big school, how he practically forced me to sit next to him in English class. I see us at fifteenth birthday parties in the local pubs, sipping coke and saying we can't wait to be older. None of them stick, they stay as moments in my mind's eye, reminding me that they aren't real anymore. I *should* have control. I *should* be able to relive these moments and not mess them up.

I keep the pain. I top it up to remind myself that he was real. I didn't make this up, I didn't lie. I remind myself that we sat in the window seat, that we shared drinks and held hands. I remind myself that even though I never said *I love you* he knew I did. I knew he loved me too. In the way he ordered my drink for me, the way he pushed apart crowds for me, the way he called me lovely and beautiful and b*est friend* every single day. He loved me in the phone calls after a night out, the Facetimes doing the dishes, the hugs that lasted a little longer and the hugs that felt like they could last forever. Somehow, I still have that naivety that forever isn't a lie. Sometimes, I think about him for so long I swear I can feel his jumper on my cheek. I often pick up the phone to text him, it usually happens when I'm at a restaurant he loved, and I want to know what to get. But now I have to make my own decisions and I don't yet like that.

*

I slide my rings back on my fingers, twisting them into place and when I look up, he is gone. The seat has disappeared from under me, and the grass is staining my jeans. There are no coffee cups in front of me, but shop bought flowers replacing wilted ones. There is no soft sunlight on my face but the first drops of rain squeezing through a growing grey cloud. He's not wearing a soft jumper, he's not holding my hand, he's not drinking coffee and singing me songs. He's not here. Not anymore.

My cheeks sting with the cold wind on my damp skin. The warmth from the memory is extinguished and replaced with a horrible guilt. A sense I have done something terribly wrong. If it is so wrong to want someone back, if it is so wrong to hate Heaven for not letting me visit, then I shall accept the name of sinner and bear its consequences. In a moment, the lightness of my heart, the parts of me that had just been so filled with reverie are trapped under the weight of a pain I cannot convey. It hurts in my head and my mouth and my knees. My arms ache, as though I am carrying around his body, but nobody can see, nobody can share the weight. Every day there is something that reminds me of him and the rope around my throat tightens until I can barely whisper his name.

But I told him I loved him. I whispered it into the wind, a hundred times over until the words lost all meaning. I say *I love you I love you I love you* as if it'll bring him back. I write his name everywhere I find a pen as if it'll write him into existence. But ink can't hold him, and my words can't reach him. I tighten my laces until I can feel my blood pulsing under the pressure. This is how my body says *we are still here.*

Next time I make us meet at the coffee shop, I'll say *I miss you.* I'll tell him about new songs and books and those people we don't like who have now broken up. I'll try and remember a different outfit he wore.

I get up, I force myself to breathe deeply. My legs feel weak, I don't have any idea how long I've been sat on the dewy grass. It's cold. My lips are chapped, and the cold makes them prickle with hints of pain. I realise I haven't said a word all day as I push my tongue around my dry mouth. I try to push away the anger; this isn't the place for anger. But there it is, so much of it. The anger at losing him and the anger at all the things I left unsaid. I feel angry for lying even if it is only in my head. I forget what is real and what is comfort these days. I am never sure of the line between *I wish,* and *I did.*

I remind myself I am alive, and I must go on living even with the gaps in me. They disappeared with him, and I don't know how to fill them. On some days, his memory feels so heavy in my arms, as though I am the sole bearer and responsible for preserving him. That weight taught me that forgetting would be murder. But I have to learn that being okay doesn't mean forgetting, but it means being free from pain and privileged with memory. I ache to the bone with the weight of learning that the day someone dies isn't the worst day of your life, but every day they stay dead is.

There are no resurrections, not in this life. No spell, potion or quantity of coffee can raise the dead.

I pull out a crinkled photograph from my back pocket and place it with the flowers. It's from that day, in the window seat. We are smiling, big wide grins.

I stand up straight, just like he did. It's one minute to four, the wardens are starting to close up the cemetery gates. I rub my eyes until I see stars; even in a cemetery I can't bear to be seen crying. I know that if there are gods above me, they are laughing at me now. For how did one young girl think she could stand in front of death and say *no*. How did I think I could convince a memory to be real again. Now that same young girl walks through empty back alleys, with tear-stained cheeks and biting her tongue. I wonder if his shadow was left behind now he's gone, I wonder if it will follow me home.

Tonight, I will write a story. I will write about the day in the window seat, and all the things I wish I had said.

The Authors

Lucy Aur

Lucy Aur is a doctoral student at Swansea university, specialising in Creative writing and Welsh history. She writes poetry and prose, both in English and Welsh, and can be found in ReSide, The Broken Spine and Lucent dreaming. Her poetry follows themes of national identity as well as confronting stigmatised topics such as grief, while her work in progress novel is a story of historical fiction; depicting Wales in the Second World War.

Outside of writing she is an avid adventurer and mental health advocate, founding her own campaign @RenegadesFoundation

Twitter: @LucyAur
Instagram: @Lucy_Aur

Sally Filer

Sally Filer is a Welsh writer and artist. She graduated from Cardiff University as a mature student with a B.A Hons in Creative Writing and English Literature in 2020. During her Masters in 2021, she tutored undergraduates and qualified to teach Creative Writing. She is currently working on her debut collection of contemporary short-stories, with a familial theme, and studying poetry online with Carol Ann Duffy, but finds her most invaluable narrative inspiration while training for half-marathons. When not writing, or running, Sally can be found creating large botanical watercolours and portraits for forthcoming exhibitions.

Instagram: @sally.filer
Facebook: Sally Filer

Elizabeth Kemball

Elizabeth Kemball is a writer from Stoke-on-Trent, now living in Wales. She studied BA English Literature and Creative Writing at the University of Warwick, and MA Creative Writing at Cardiff University. Her poetry and prose have been featured in various online and print magazines and journals such as Black Bough, Ink Sweat & Tears, and Variant Literature. Her micro-chapbook 'A letter from your sheets // if your sheets could speak.' was published by Nightingale & Sparrow Press in March 2020. Her work often focuses on folklore, myth, and magic. She is currently working on her debut novel about witchcraft and revenge.

Twitter: @LizzieKemball
Instagram: @lizziekemball
Bookstagram: @devouring.words

Bethany Lewis

Bethany Lewis is writer from Merthyr Tydfil. She has an MA in Creative Writing from Cardiff University.

Bethany loves writing historical fiction with a focus on women's stories. She is currently penning her debut novel, a tale exploring themes of ambition, freedom, and betrayal set in Renaissance Florence. She also likes to experiment with short stories and flash fiction, and can even be found scrawling the occasional poem into her notes app.

In her spare time, Bethany runs a bookstagram account, @tiny_library_, documenting her writing journey, reviewing books, and sharing her own writing tips with a community of book lovers.

Twitter: @_Bethany_Lewis
Instagram: @bethanylewis_x
Bookstagram: @_tinylibrary_

Advanced Praise

'Tales of cursed poets, speaking statues, troublesome tapestries and nostalgia for lost love combine in this vibrant quartet, in which the magical pervades the everyday. Each of these four stories, in their different ways, offers witty and assured writing, with flecks of wisdom.'
Richard Gwyn, author of *The Blue Tent*

'A blazingly imaginative introduction to four hugely talented new writers, their voices urgent, original, and contemporary.'
Alan Bilton, author of *The End of The Yellow House*

'In Four Forked Tongues, four skilled writers spin their stories like silk. Intriguing, surreal and filled with magic, these tales challenge the reader to question what they think they know, to look a little deeper, and to reconsider the art of storytelling.'
Mari Ellis Dunning, author of *Pearl & Bone*

'The Broken Spine deliver another exciting publication; this time a collection of four distinctive female writers with compelling, unsettling narratives, where the style and atmosphere of Jeanette Winterson's writing and Roald Dahl's Tales of the Unexpected potently converge.'
Matthew M. C. Smith, author of *The Keeper of Aeons*; editor of *Black Bough Poetry*

Recommended Reading

Anthologies

The Broken Spine Artist Collective: First Edition (2020)
The Broken Spine Artist Collective: Second Edition (2020)
The Broken Spine Artist Collective: Third Edition (2021)
The Broken Spine Artist Collective: Fourth Edition (2022)
The Broken Spine Artist Collective: Fifth Edition (2022)
BOLD: An anthology of masculinity themed creative writing (2023)

Chapbooks

Neon Ghosts (A. Parry, 2020)
The Mask (E. Horan, 2021)
Holy Things (J. Rafferty, 2022)
From This Soil (C. Bailey, 2022)
The Keeper of Aeons (M. M. C. Smith, 2022)

Printed in Great Britain
by Amazon